S0-CFJ-963

Jellyfish Role

Kelly Doudna

Illustrated by Neena Chawla

Consulting Editor, Diane Craig, M.A./Reading Specialist

ABDO
Publishing Company

Published by ABDO Publishing Company, 4940 Viking Drive, Edina, Minnesota 55435.

Copyright © 2007 by Abdo Consulting Group, Inc. International copyrights reserved in all countries. No part of this book may be reproduced in any form without written permission from the publisher. SandCastle™ is a trademark and logo of ABDO Publishing Company.

Printed in the United States.

Credits
Edited by: Pam Price
Curriculum Coordinator: Nancy Tuminelly
Cover and Interior Design and Production: Mighty Media
Photo Credits: Ross Armstrong/SeaPics.com, Scott Leslie/SeaPics.com, Masa Ushioda/SeaPics.com, David Wrobel/SeaPics.com, ShutterStock

Library of Congress Cataloging-in-Publication Data

Doudna, Kelly, 1963-
    Jellyfish role / Kelly Doudna; illustrated by Neena Chawla.
        p. cm. -- (Fact & fiction. Critter chronicles)
    Summary: Jenny Jellyfish wins the starring role in her school play. Alternating pages provide facts about jellyfish.
    ISBN 10 1-59928-446-4 (hardcover)
    ISBN 10 1-59928-447-2 (paperback)

    ISBN 13 978-1-59928-446-0 (hardcover)
    ISBN 13 978-1-59928-447-7 (paperback)
    [1. Theater--Fiction. 2. Jellyfishes--Fiction.] I. Chawla, Neena, ill. II. Title. III. Series.

    PZ7.D74425Jel 2006
    [E]--dc22

                                                                                              2006005541

SandCastle Level: Fluent

SandCastle™ books are created by a professional team of educators, reading specialists, and content developers around five essential components—phonemic awareness, phonics, vocabulary, text comprehension, and fluency—to assist young readers as they develop reading skills and strategies and increase their general knowledge. All books are written, reviewed, and leveled for guided reading, early reading intervention, and Accelerated Reader® programs for use in shared, guided, and independent reading and writing activities to support a balanced approach to literacy instruction. The SandCastle™ series has four levels that correspond to early literacy development. The levels help teachers and parents select appropriate books for young readers.

Emerging Readers
(no flags)

Beginning Readers
(1 flag)

Transitional Readers
(2 flags)

Fluent Readers
(3 flags)

These levels are meant only as a guide. All levels are subject to change.

FACT & FiCTiON

This series provides early fluent readers the opportunity to develop reading comprehension strategies and increase fluency. These books are appropriate for guided, shared, and independent reading.

FACT The left-hand pages incorporate realistic photographs to enhance readers' understanding of informational text.

FiCTiON The right-hand pages engage readers with an entertaining, narrative story that is supported by whimsical illustrations.

The Fact and Fiction pages can be read separately to improve comprehension through questioning, predicting, making inferences, and summarizing. They can also be read side-by-side, in spreads, which encourages students to explore and examine different writing styles.

FACT OR **FiCTiON?** This fun quiz helps reinforce students' understanding of what is real and not real.

SPEED READ The text-only version of each section includes word-count rulers for fluency practice and assessment.

GLOSSARY Higher-level vocabulary and concepts are defined in the glossary.

SandCastle™ would like to hear from you.

Tell us your stories about reading this book. What was your favorite page? Was there something hard that you needed help with? Share the ups and downs of learning to read. To get posted on the ABDO Publishing Company Web site, send us an e-mail at:

sandcastle@abdopublishing.com

Jellyfish are not fish. They are invertebrates with no head, brain, heart, or bones. They are 95 percent water.

Jenny Jellyfish is trying out for the school play. This year, the school is performing *The Jelly of Oz*. It's a play about Dottie the jellyfish's adventures in the waters around Australia.

Jellyfish have umbrella- or globe-shaped bells. They also have a large number of tentacles, which may be long or short.

Fiction

After the audition, Jenny says nervously to her friend Lionel, "I was such a blob. I probably won't even be cast as a flying sea monkey."

7

The lion's mane jellyfish is the largest
jellyfish. Its bell is up to eight feet wide.
Its tentacles can reach 100 feet.

The cast list is posted. Jenny exclaims, "I can't believe I get to play the lead role of Dottie!" Lionel has been cast as the cowardly lion's mane jellyfish. Rehearsals begin the next day.

Jellyfish move by floating on ocean currents. Some jellyfish contract the muscles in their bells to move themselves.

In the play, Dottie and her friends
pulse through the water and sing,
"Follow the Jelly Brick Road. Follow
the Jelly Brick Road." Dottie carries
her pet dogfish, Tiger, in a basket.

11

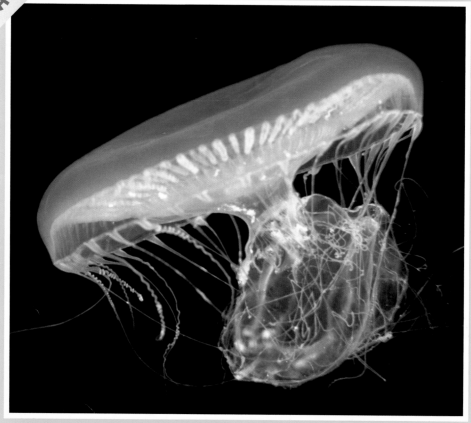

Jellyfish are predators. Some jellyfish even catch and eat other jellyfish.

Dottie, the cowardly lion's mane, and the others float along the Jelly Brick Road. They have almost reached Oz when they meet the Wicked Witch of the Sea. The witch reaches out to grab Dottie.

Some sea creatures are not harmed by jellyfish and will swim into their bells or tentacles to avoid other predators.

Dottie is swept away
from the Wicked Witch of
the Sea by a strong current. The witch
wiggles her tentacles at Dottie and cries,
"I'll get you, my jelly, and your
little dogfish too!"

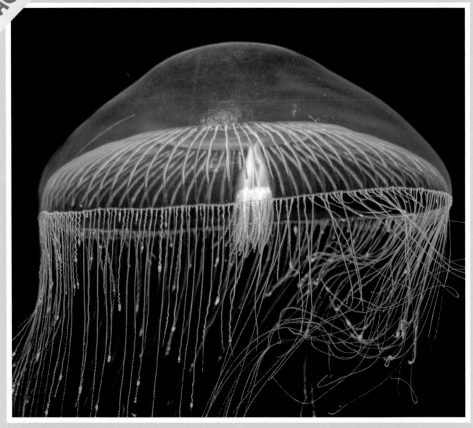

Many jellyfish species contain chemicals that cause them to light up.

Dottie spies a glow behind a coral reef. It's the wizard. Dottie asks, "Wizard, would you please tell me how to get home?"

The wizard answers in a kind voice, "Just click your tentacles together and keep repeating, 'There's no place like home.'"

Jellyfish are found in all the world's oceans, from shallow waters near shore to deep in the oceans.

Dottie wakes up safe in her own bed. She exclaims, "So I was knocked out when I was spun around in a giant whirlpool? The whole adventure was a dream? There *is* no place like home!"

As the curtain comes down, Jenny, Lionel, and the other actors take a bow. The audience shouts bravo!

Fiction

FACT OR FICTION?

Read each statement below. Then decide whether it's from the FACT section or the FICTION section!

  1. Jellyfish are not fish.

  2. Jellyfish audition for plays.

  3. Jellyfish carry pets in baskets.

  4. Jellyfish are found in all the world's oceans.

ANSWERS
1. fact 2. fiction 3. fiction 4. fact

Jellyfish are not fish. They are invertebrates with no head, brain, heart, or bones. They are 95 percent water.

Jellyfish have umbrella- or globe-shaped bells. They also have a large number of tentacles, which may be long or short.

The lion's mane jellyfish is the largest jellyfish. Its bell is up to eight feet wide. Its tentacles can reach 100 feet.

Jellyfish move by floating on ocean currents. Some jellyfish contract the muscles in their bells to move themselves.

Jellyfish are predators. Some jellyfish even catch and eat other jellyfish.

Some sea creatures are not harmed by jellyfish and will swim into their bells or tentacles to avoid other predators.

Many jellyfish species contain chemicals that cause them to light up.

Jellyfish are found in all the world's oceans, from shallow waters near shore to deep in the oceans.

Jenny Jellyfish is trying out for the school play. 9
This year, the school is performing *The Jelly of Oz*. 19
It's a play about Dottie the jellyfish's adventures 27
in the waters around Australia. 32

After the audition, Jenny says nervously to her 40
friend Lionel, "I was such a blob. I probably 49
won't even be cast as a flying sea monkey." 58

The cast list is posted. Jenny exclaims, "I can't 67
believe I get to play the lead role of Dottie!" 77
Lionel has been cast as the cowardly lion's mane 86
jellyfish. Rehearsals begin the next day. 92

In the play, Dottie and her friends pulse 100
through the water and sing, "Follow the Jelly 108
Brick Road. Follow the Jelly Brick Road." Dottie 116
carries her pet dogfish, Tiger, in a basket. 124

Dottie, the cowardly lion's mane, and the others 132
float along the Jelly Brick Road. They have almost 141
reached Oz when they meet the Wicked Witch of 150
the Sea. The witch reaches out to grab Dottie. 159

Dottie is swept away from the Wicked Witch of the Sea by a strong current. The witch wiggles her tentacles at Dottie and cries, "I'll get you, my jelly, and your little dogfish too!"

Dottie spies a glow behind a coral reef. It's the wizard. Dottie asks, "Wizard, would you please tell me how to get home?"

The wizard answers in a kind voice, "Just click your tentacles together and keep repeating, 'There's no place like home.'"

Dottie wakes up safe in her own bed. She exclaims, "So I was knocked out when I was spun around in a giant whirlpool? The whole adventure was a dream? There *is* no place like home!"

As the curtain comes down, Jenny, Lionel, and the other actors take a bow. The audience shouts bravo!

GLOSSARY

audition. a tryout for a role in a performance

cast. 1) to give an actor a role in a performance
2) a group of actors who perform together

contract. to squeeze together and become smaller

current. steady flow of movement in a liquid or a gas

invertebrate. a creature that does not have a spine

Oz. a nickname for Australia

predator. an animal that hunts others

rehearsal. a practice session before a performance

role. a part played by an actor

tentacle. a long, flexible limb on an invertebrate
such as a jellyfish, octopus, or squid

To see a complete list of SandCastle™ books and other nonfiction titles from
ABDO Publishing Company, visit www.abdopublishing.com or contact us at:
4940 Viking Drive, Edina, Minnesota 55435 • 1-800-800-1312 • fax: 1-952-831-1632

Edison Twp. Free Public Library
North Edison Branch
777 Grove Ave
Edison, New Jersey 08820

AUG 1 7 2016